LES MISÉRABLES

LES MISÉRABLES

Victor Hugo

Om Books International

Om Books International

Reprinted in 2024

Corporate & Editorial Office
A-12, Sector 64, Noida 201 301
Uttar Pradesh, India
Phone: +91 120 477 4100
Email: editorial@ombooks.com
Website: www.ombooksinternational.com

Sales Office
107, Ansari Road, Darya Ganj
New Delhi 110 002, India
Phone: +91 11 4000 9000
Email: sales@ombooks.com
Website: www.ombooks.com

Abridged by Swayam Ganguly

ISBN: 978-93-85031-55-7

Printed in China

10 9 8 7 6 5 4 3 2

Contents

Chapter One

The Tramp

An hour before sunset on October 1815, a man travelling by foot entered the little town of D____. The few who were at their windows or doors, viewed this person with distrust. He was wretched in appearance, a stout and hardy man of middle height and around forty-six or seven years old. His face was half obscured by a slouched leather cap, sweaty and bronzed by the sun and wind. The coarse yellow shirt was partially unbuttoned, revealing his shaggy chest and a small silver anchor was fastened at the neck. His hair was cropped but he sported

a long beard. The man wore a cravat twisted like a rope and worn out, shabby blue trousers, white on one knee, with holes in the other. His old, ragged gray blouse was patched on one side with a piece of green cloth sewed with twine. He carried a heavy knapsack on his back, strongly buckled and new. His hand held a huge knotted stick and his feet were stockingless with hobnailed shoes.

As no one knew him, he was obviously a traveller. But where had he come from? From the South? Perhaps from the sea? For, he was entering D___ by the same road, which the Emperor Napoleon had travelled by, from Cannes to Paris. This man must have walked all day long as he seemed exhausted. Some women of the old city, located at the lower part of town, had spotted him take a break under the trees of the Boulevard Gassendi, drinking from the fountain at the end of the promenade. It was obvious he was thirsty as the children spied

him, having a drink again at the fountain in the market place, just two hundred steps away.

The man took a left turn after reaching the corner of the Rue Poichevert and headed towards the mayor's office. He entered, to come out after a quarter of an hour, raising his cap humbly to salute a gendarme seated near the door. A good inn called *La Croix de Colbas,* existed in D___ at that time. The host was called Jacquin Labarre, a man held in high esteem in town. The traveller entered the kitchen of the inn that opened out to the street.

"What will monsieur have?" the host asked without raising his eyes from his ranges.

"Something to eat and lodging."

"Nothing is as easy," the host is declared and then observing the stranger closely, adding "For pay."

"I have money," the stranger replied withdrawing a large leather purse from his pocket.

"I am at your service then," the host replied.

Putting his purse back into his pocket and setting down his knapsack by the door, the stranger sat on a low stool by the fire, holding his stick. As D___ was located in the mountains, the October evenings were cold.

The host carefully kept his eyes on the traveller, as he passed back and forth. He scribbled on a scrap of paper with a pencil as the guest had his back towards him. He handed the scrap of paper to a child who appeared to be both his lackey and scullion. After a whisper, the boy ran off to the mayor's office.

"Is dinner ready?" the traveller asked again.

"In a few moments," the host replied.

The boy returned with the paper soon and the host opened it hurriedly. He read attentively and thought for a while. Then he approached the traveller who seemed absorbed in troubled thought.

"I cannot receive you Monsieur," the host declared.

"Why?" the traveller asked, half rising from his seat. "Are you afraid I won't pay you? Do you want advance payment? I have money!"

"It's not that. I have no room."

"Put me in the stable then," the man stated quietly.

"The horses take all the room there."

"Well, a corner in the garret then; a truss of straw. We will see about that after dinner."

"I cannot give you any dinner," the host declared firmly. The traveller protested but the host refused to relent stating that all the rooms had been taken by the wagoners. The traveller refused to leave and was startled when the host bent down to whisper in a hiss, "Go away! Shall I tell you your name? It is Jean Valjean! Shall I tell you who you are? I suspected something was wrong when I spotted you enter and sent word to the mayor's office. Here is the reply," he thrust a paper towards the traveller, who read it. Then the traveller collected his knapsack and left

the inn. He entered a tavern in the Rue Chaffaut but was turned out from there as well. It so happened that a fisherman residing there had spotted what had happened at the other inn and had informed the innkeeper.

The traveller enquired at the prison if he would be allowed to spend the night there.

"A prison is not a tavern. Get yourself arrested first," was the reply. The man entered a small street with many gardens. He spotted a pretty little one-story house, with a light at a window. He peeped in to see a forty year old peasant at the table, with his wife and two children. There was food and wine on the table, and the family was laughing. The man rapped on the window thrice, before he was heard, and the door opened.

"Monsieur, I beg your pardon," he stated. "Can you give me a plate of soup and a corner in your garden shed to sleep in? I shall pay."

"But why don't you go to the inn?" the peasant enquired.

"There is no room."

"That's impossible. Have you been to Labarre's house or the place in Rue Chaffaut?"

"They didn't take me."

"Are you the man?" the peasant exclaimed suddenly with a shudder. He stepped back, and took down his gun from the wall. His wife grabbed the children, seeking refuge behind her husband. "Get out!" the peasant ordered as if the man was a snake. "A glass of water, for pity's sake," the man pleaded but the door was slammed shut on his face. The heavy bolts were drawn, and the windows were shut and barred. As night fell, the man spotted a small hut in one of the gardens. He cleared a wooden fence to enter the garden. The small hut was actually a dog-kennel and the man had just entered the hut to lie down, when he saw a huge bull dog at the door. Making a shield of his stick and knapsack, the man somehow managed to escape. He tramped out of town now, to arrive in a field. He retraced his steps. The gates of D____ were closed now but the old walls flanking the city had breaches in them from sieges in the religious wars. The man entered the town through a breach.

It was eight in the evening. The man passed the prefecture, the seminary and then the Cathedral Square, shaking his fist at the church. A printing office stands at the corner of this square. The proclamations of the emperor were printed here first, as well as the Imperial Guard to the army, brought from the island of Elba and dictated by Napoleon himself. Extremely fatigued, the man threw himself on a stone bench here. An old woman exited the church just then and asked him what he was doing there. The man replied harshly that he was going to sleep.

"Upon the bench?" the good woman asked. "I've had a wooden mattress for nineteen years. Tonight I have a stone one," he replied.

"You've been a soldier?"

"Yes."

The woman asked him why he didn't go to an inn. He lied that he didn't have any money. She gave him the four sous she had in her purse. "You cannot find lodging for so less," she stated. "But try to get lodging for charity."

"Everyone has driven me away!"

"Have you knocked at that door there?" the woman pointed.

"No!"

"Knock there!"

Chapter Two

The Convict meets the Bishop

The Bishop of D___ preferred to remain in his room till late, after his evening walk in town. He was busy with his great work on Duty, which was still incomplete. He was still at work at eight o'clock when Madam Magloire arrived as usual, to take the silver from the panel near the bed. The Bishop left for the dining room a little later where his sister had just placed the plates. Madam Magloire was in conversation with Mademoiselle Baptistine and the last thing they spoke about when the Bishop entered was the suspicious vagabond lurking about town. There was talk as to how everyone should

secure their doors at night. "Are we in great danger?" he asked in good humor.

"It is true, monsieur. Everyone says something will happen tonight in town. The police are so badly organized and we do not even have proper street lamps," Madame Magloire declared. She asked the Bishop's permission to fetch the locksmith to replace the old bolts on the door. At that very moment, there was a violent knock on the door.

"Come in!" the Bishop said.

The door opened wide and rather quickly, as if pushed by someone possessing energy and boldness. A man entered and paused, leaving the door behind him open. He held a stick in his hand, and a knapsack on his back. His face appeared haggard and hideous as seen by the firelight, almost an apparition of ill-omen. Madame Magloire was petrified and trembled with her mouth open. The man spoke loudly, "My name is Jean Valjean and

I am a convict! I have spent nineteen years in the galleys and was set free four days ago. I started for my destination, Pontarlier, walking four days from Toulon. I have walked twelve leagues today. I was turned away from an inn here because of my yellow passport, which I had displayed at the mayor's office as was necessary. No inn would have me and neither would the prison. I was chased away from a dog kennel by a dog as if he were a man! I lay upon a stone in the square and a good lady showed me your house. 'Knock there!' she said and I have done so. Is this an inn? I have money. My savings of one hundred and nine francs and fifteen sous, earned in the galleys for the work of nineteen years. I am tired and hungry. Can I stay?"

"Madame Magloire," the Bishop instructed. "Put on another plate."

The man took three steps to reach near the lamp on the table. "Stop!" he exclaimed, as if fearful he hadn't been heard. "I am a galley slave, didn't you hear? A convict just from the galleys. There is my passport, yellow as you can see," he said, withdrawing a large yellow paper from his pocket. "It's enough to have me kicked out from wherever I enter. Will you read it? I know how to read, having learnt in the galleys at a school. Read what they have put here: *'Jean Valjean, a liberated convict, native of_____, has been nineteen years in the galleys; five years for burglary; fourteen years for having attempted to escape four times. This man is very dangerous.'*

There you have it! Will you receive me? Is this an inn? Can you give me something to eat and a place to sleep? Do you have a stable?"

"Madame Magloire," the Bishop instructed. "Put some sheets on the bed in the alcove."

As she left, the Bishop addressed the man, "Monsieur, sit down and warm yourself. We shall take supper presently and your bed will be made ready while you sup."

As realization finally dawned, the man's hard and gloomy expression changed to one of doubt and joy. He stammered like a madman, "What? Is it true? You won't drive me away? You call a convict *Monsieur* and don't say 'Get out, dog!' like everyone else. Oh! The fine woman who sent me here. I shall finally have supper and a bed like other people with mattress and sheets. A bed! I haven't slept in one for nineteen years. You are good people! Monsieur Innkeeper, what is your name? I will pay all you say. You are a fine man. You are an innkeeper?"

"I am a priest living here," the Bishop replied.

"Oh, noble priest. How stupid I am not to notice your cap," the man stated as he sat down. Mademoiselle Baptistine looked at him pleasantly. "You don't want me to pay?" the man enquired.

"No, keep your money," the Bishop replied. Madame Magloire fetched a plate to set it on the table. Each time the Bishop addressed the man as Monsieur, his face lit up. *Monsieur* to a convict is similar to a glass of water to a man dying of thirst at sea. “You do not need to thank me,” the Bishop said to the man. “This is the house of Christ. You are welcome here as you are suffering, hungry and thirsty. Besides, I knew your name before you told me,” he stated to the surprised man. “You have seen much suffering?”

“Oh, the red blouse, the ball and chain, the plank as a bed, the heat, the cold, the crew of the galley, the lash, the double chain, the dungeon for a word and the chain even when sick in bed. The dogs are happier! Nineteen years! Now I am forty-six, with a yellow passport.”

“Remember that there is joy in heaven over the tears of a repentant sinner than over the white robes of a hundred good men,” the Bishop stated. “If you leave that sorrowful place with goodwill and peace rather than hate and anger against men, you are better than all of us.”

Supper was served, comprising of soup, bread, a little pork, a mutton scrap, figs, green cheese and a large loaf of rye bread. A bottle of fine old Mauves wine was added by Madame Magloire. The Bishop was happy. "To supper!" he exclaimed, out of habit whenever he was entertaining a guest. The stranger was seated at his right, while Mademoiselle Baptistine took her natural place at his left. The Bishop said the blessing and served the soup himself, as his usual custom. The man ate greedily.

"Monsieur, I will show you to your room," Monseigneur Bienvenu stated to his guest, after having said goodnight to his sister. The man followed him and as they passed the Bishop's sleeping chamber, Madame Magloire was putting up the silver in the cupboard at the end of the bed. This was the last thing she did each night before going to bed. The Bishop deposited his guest in the alcove and bid him goodnight. The stranger thanked the Bishop and suddenly

made a singular motion, which would have horrified the two women in the house had they witnessed it. It is difficult to assume why he did it. Was he throwing a warning or did he do so on impulse?

"You lodge me in your house, as near as that!" he said harshly, adding with a laugh. "I could be a murderer."

"God will take care of that," the Bishop responded and blessed the man who, however, did not bow. The stranger was so tired that he blew out the candle with his nostril just like convicts do and fell on the bed fully dressed. As he fell into deep sleep, the clock struck midnight and the Bishop returned to his chamber.

Chapter Three

Convicted

Jean Valjean was born of a poor peasant family. He had not been taught to read and chose the occupation of a pruner when he grew up. He lost both parents when young, and had only one living relative in his sister. She was a widow with seven children, and had taken care of her younger brother till her husband was alive. But when her husband died, leaving behind the eighth child, that was one year old, a twenty-five year old Jean Valjean supported the sister who had raised him. His youth was spent in hard labour, and he never had the time to fall in love.

In the pruning season, he earned eighteen sous a day and then he hired himself out as a workman, reaper or laborer, doing whatever work came his way. His sister worked as well, having eight children to feed. Misery crept upon this sad group slowly and after a particularly severe winter, the family had no bread!

One Sunday night, Maubert Isabeau, the baker on the Place de 1'Eglise in Faverolles was about to go to bed when he heard a violent blow against his barred shop window. He rushed down to spot an arm seize a loaf of bread through the broken glass. Isbaueu chased the thief and caught him. The thief had thrown away the bread but his arm was still bleeding. The thief was Jean Valjean and the year was 1795. Jean Valjean was produced before the tribunals, found guilty and sentenced to five years in the galleys.

He wept as heavy hammer-strokes behind his head riveted the bolt of his iron collar. He

was taken to Toulon, after a journey of twenty-five days on a cart, the chain around his neck. He was dressed in a red blouse at Toulon and his past life, including his name was erased. He was no longer Jean Valjean: he was Number 24,601.

At the end of his fourth year, his comrades helped him escape but he was retaken on the evening of the second day. His sentence was extended for three years for this escape attempt, which made eight. He tried escaping again in his sixth year and failed again. An addition of five years was made to his sentence, two with the double chain. That made his sentence thirteen years. He tried escaping on his tenth year, failed and three more years were added. Sixteen years! In his thirteenth year, his escape plan was thwarted yet again and his sentence went up to nineteen years now. Jean Valjean was finally set free in October, 1815. He had entered prison nineteen years ago in 1796, for breaking

FOREMAN

a pane of glass and stealing a loaf of bread. He had entered the galleys sobbing and exited as a hardened, sullen man.

The words 'You are free!' seemed strange and unreal to his ears when they were uttered and Jean Valjean was dazzled with the idea of freedom. But the new life he had expected, faded just like his yellow passport. The day after he was liberated, he offered his services to people loading bags at an orange flower distillery at Grasse and was accepted. The foreman was satisfied with his work, but he was paid only half the wages he had earned on account of his yellow passport. "That is good enough for you," the foreman had declared. "Watch out for the lock-up!" he had added, when Jean Valjean had insisted for his fair share of wages. The state and society had robbed him by wholesale and now, the individual was robbing him by retail. Liberation is not deliverance. A convict leaves the gallows behind but not his condemnation.

Chapter Four

Robberies

Jean Valjean awoke when the cathedral clock struck two. It was a bed that was too good that woke him up. He was sleeping in a proper bed after twenty years and the sensation was too novel not to disturb his sleep. One thought dominated his mind; the six silver plates and the large ladle that the woman had put on the table. His mind was lost in thought and in an inner conflict for an hour. But when the clock struck three, he sat up on his bed. Then, he walked up to the window and discovered that it had no bars, and opened out into the garden. He returned to his knapsack and took out a

short iron bar, pointed at one end like a spear. It looked like a lever or a club but was actually a miner's drill, used by convicts to quarry stones on the hills. It was made of solid iron, ending in a point at the lower end, to sink into the rock easily. He took the drill and moved towards the Bishop's room, which was unlocked.

Jean Valjean pushed the door like a cat and then more forcefully. He passed through the opening, pushing the door open wider. There was a harsh creak from the rusty hinge and he trembled. But no one stirred in the house. Soon, Jean Valjean had reached the bed and saw the Bishop sleeping peacefully. He saw the Bishop smiling in his sleep. Then suddenly, he made for the cupboard, raised his drill and forced open the lock. Taking the basket of silver, he left the room to enter the oratory. He collected his things, shoved the silver in his knapsack, threw away the basket and ran across the garden. Leaping over the wall like a tiger, Jean Valjean fled.

The next day, the theft was discovered by Madame Magloire's cry.

"That abominable fellow has stolen our silver," she informed the Bishop angrily.

"Now first, did this silver belong to us?" the Bishop enquired mildly. "It belonged to the poor and this man was poor evidently. I have wrongly withheld this silver till now."

After some time, they were seated at the breakfast table, when there was a knock on the door.

"Come in," the Bishop said and four strange men entered. Three were gendarmes, holding a fourth by the caller. He was Jean Valjean.

The brigadier approached the Bishop with a military salute. "Monseigneur," he began and Jean Valjean tried to say something.

"Silence before the Bishop," the brigadier ordered.

"I am happy to see you," the Bishop said to Jean Valjean. "But I gave you silver candlesticks as well, that would have fetched two hundred francs. Why didn't you take them with the plates?"

""Monseigneur, does this man speak the truth then?" the brigadier enquired. "We arrested him with this silver."

"It is a mistake," the Bishop stated.

"Can we let him go then?"

"Certainly."

The gendarmes released Jean Valjean, who couldn't believe his luck. "Take your candlesticks before you leave, my friend," the Bishop said to him. A trembling Jean Valjean took the candlesticks.

"Go in peace!" the Bishop said, and Jean Valjean felt as if he would faint. The gendarmes left and the Bishop addressed the convict, "Remember that you have promised to use this silver to become an honest man. My brother, you do not belong to evil any more but to good. I am buying your soul for you. I withdraw it from dark thoughts and I give it to God."

Jean Valjean escaped from the city without realizing that he was actually retracing his steps. He wandered about on empty stomach all morning. As the sun set he spotted a small Savoyard, about twelve years old, coming down the path. He was singing with his hurdy-gurdy at his side and his marmot box on his back. The boy was one of those happy youngsters who wander from one place to the other, singing for money. He was tossing up pieces of money that he had made as he walked and catching them. One of the coins, a forty sous piece escaped him, and rolled near Jean Valjean who put his foot over it. The boy came up and asked for his coin.

"What is your name?" Jean Valjean asked.

"Petit Gervais, monsieur."

"Get out!"

"Give me my piece, monsieur," the boy demanded. He shook Jean Valjean by the collar of his blouse and tried to dislodge his foot from his treasure.

"You better take care of yourself," Jean Valjean stared threateningly at the boy and said. The boy shook in terror and ran away sobbing.

The sun had set and Jean Valjean was very weak, not having eaten all day. He was feverish and shivered in the cold night air. He suddenly picked up the forty sous piece under his foot and looked at the direction the boy had run. He went in that direction, calling out the boy's name. "Petit Gervais!" he cried repeatedly but there was no reply. He met a priest on horseback who hadn't seen the boy either. Jean Valjean donated two five-franc pieces for the poor by handing them to the priest who fled fearfully after Jean Valjean confessed that he was a robber.

All efforts to locate the boy failed and Jean Valjean burst into tears. He cried for the first time in nineteen years. As he wept, the light grew brighter and clearer in his own mind. All the events of his past life flashed before

him, including the latest events but in a light never seen before. His life appeared horrible to him and his soul, frightful. It appeared that he was looking at Satan through the light of Paradise. No one knows how long he wept or where he went but at three in the morning, the stage-driver who passed through the bishop's street saw a man praying, kneeling upon the pavement before the Monseigneur Bishop's door.

TO THE SERGEANT
OF
WATERLOO

Chapter Five

Fantine meets the Thenardiers

A sort of chop house once existed at Montfermeil, near Paris. It was kept by a husband and wife named Thenardier and located in the Lane Boulanger. A board was nailed over the door, featuring a painting, representing a battle. The inscription below it said: TO THE SERGEANT OF WATERLOO.

The vehicle or rather the fragment of the vehicle obstructing the street in front of the Sergeant of Waterloo one evening in the spring of 1815, was the fore-carriage used for transporting heavy articles and was made up of a gigantic iron axle tree with a pivot that had a heavy pole attached to it. It was supported by two huge wheels and resembled a massive gun-carriage. A huge chain fit for the Goliath of the galleys, hung under the axle-tree.

That evening, two little girls used this chain as a swinging rope. The eighteen month child was on the lap of the two and a half year old. The mother sat on the sill of the inn, swinging the two children by a long string, her careful eyes on them all the time. The creaking noises of the chain resonated with the ecstatic cries of the children as they were swung. Nothing would have made a more pleasant sight with the setting sun mingling in the picture. A woman stood at a distance, bearing a child in her arms and carrying a large, heavy carpet bag. The child aged two or three in this woman's arms, was the divinest little thing wearing a head-dress of fine linen with ribbons adorning her shoulders and Valenciennes lace on her cap. She appeared a rosy and healthy child and was sleeping.

"My name is Madame Thenardier," the mother of the two girls said. "We keep this inn."

She was a red-haired, brawny, thirty year old woman armed with a masculine laziness. The traveller said she was a working woman with a dead husband. Unable to seek work in Paris, she was leaving for her own province to look for it. She had left Paris that morning on foot and carrying the child had tired her. She had boarded the Villemomble stage and had come walking to Montfermeil. The child had walked a little and had fallen asleep. She kissed her daughter and she woke up, surveying the world with her pretty little eyes. Then she laughed and after spotting the two children swinging, put out her tongue admiringly. Madame Thenardier untied her children from the swing and asked the three to play together. Acquaintance is easy at that age and the two women chatted as the children played. "What do you call your brat?"

"Cosette."

"How old is she?"

"Going on three years."

"The age of my oldest one. Look how soon they become friends. One would think they were three sisters."

These words were the very spark the other woman was seeking. "Will you keep my child for me?" she pleaded, surprising Madame Thenardier. "I cannot take my child into the country," the mother explained. "Work forbids that I could find a place there with a child. God has led me to your inn and my daughter will be with sisters and a mother here. It will not be long before I return."

"Let me think over it," Madame Thenardier replied.

"I shall pay six francs a month."

"Nothing less than seven francs and six months payment in advance," a man's voice

was heard from within. "That's forty two francs," Madame Thenardier declared.

"I shall give it," the woman said. "Fifteen francs extra for initial expenses," the man added. "That's fifty seven francs," his wife declared.

"I shall give it. I have just eighty francs. That leaves me with enough to walk to the country. I shall earn some money there and return for my love."

"Does the child have a wardrobe?" the man enquired.

"Yes, she has a fine wardrobe just like a lady. In my carpet bag."

The man appeared and asked her to leave the bag behind as well. The bargain was struck and the mother spent the night at the inn to leave the next morning. A neighbour met her on the way, and reported her crying as if her heart had broken. Fantine had been deceived by the man she had loved, who hadn't married her as he had promised after a child was born to them.

"That will help me repay my note of hundred and ten francs which is due tomorrow," the man declared to his wife. "I was fifty francs short. You have proved to be a good mousetrap with your little ones."

"Without even knowing it," his wife replied.

The captured mouse was tiny but yet the cat exulted. The Thenardiers belonged to that bastard class formed of low people who have risen and intelligent people who have fallen. This class existed between the middle and the lower class and some of the faults of the latter united with all the vices of the former. They did not possess either the generosity of the workman or the respectability of the bourgeois. Thenardier if he may be believed, claimed to be a soldier, a sergeant from the campaign of 1815. The sign of his inn reflected his feats of arms and he had painted it himself, as he knew how to do a bit of everything, albeit badly.

But prosperity is not guaranteed by being wicked and the inn was not a success. Thanks to Fantine's fifty seven francs, the Thenardiers' survived and when that was exhausted the woman took Cosette's wardrobe to town and pawned it for sixty francs. Then, they dressed the child in rags and fed her with leftovers. Cosette ate with the dog and the cat under the table, in a wooden dish. The mother had found a place at M____, and enquired about her child. She was told that Cosette was doing well and she sent seven francs for the seventh month. Thenardier wrote back, demanding twelve francs and the poor woman agreed, thinking her daughter was well taken care of.

The woman and her girls, Eponine and Azelma, were unkind to Cosette. Little girls are but copies of their mother, just the size that is reduced. Two years passed by, and people

praised the Thenardiers for raising a child that was not their own. Thenardier had learnt from his sources that the child was probably illegitimate and now demanded fifteen francs a month from the mother who agreed. As Cosette grew up, so did her misery. She was reduced to the servant of the house when she was five. It was heart wrenching to see the six year old shiver under her tattered dress in the chills of winter, sweeping the street with a large broom in her little hands and tears in her eyes. She was nicknamed the Lark, not bigger than a bird, trembling and frightened, first to wake up in the village. Only the poor lark never sang!

Chapter Six

Father Madeleine

Fantine arrived at M____ in 1818. Fantine had left the province twelve years ago and it had changed vastly in appearance. While Fantine had sunk deeper into misery, her native village had risen to prosperity, thanks to industrial changes. For a long time, the specialized occupation of the village had been the imitation of English jets and German black glass trinkets. The business had always been dull because of the high price of the raw material. But at the end of 1815, a stranger had established himself here and had conceived the idea of substituting gum-lac for resin in the manufacturing process.

For bracelets particularly, he created the clasps just by bending the ends of the metal together, instead of soldering them.

This slight change had created a revolution. The price of the raw material had reduced considerably and the wages of the laborer went up. The quality of the goods were improved, a benefit for the consumer and the manufacturer sold them at a lower price and yet made thrice the profit. It was good that the inventor had made all around him rich as well. No one knew the history of this stranger but people said he came to this town as a laborer, with a few hundred francs to make a fortune for himself as well as the region. The December evening he had entered the city with a stick in his hand and a bundle on his back, a great fire had broken out. The man had charged into the fire and saved two children by risking his own life. These were the children of the captain of the gendarmerie and in the gratitude of the moment, no one asked the man for his passport. He was known from that day as Father Madeleine.

Father Madeleine was about fifty, good-natured and always preoccupied in thought. He employed everyone, on the condition that they be honest. He thought much for others and little for himself. In 1820, it was revealed that he had six hundred and thirty thousand francs in the bank. But he had spent more than a million for the city and for the poor. He was a religious man and in 1819, under the recommendation of the prefect, he was appointed Mayor of M____ by the king. But he declined this offer. The king conferred upon him the Cross of the Legion of Honor that was also declined. Everyone was forced to honor and love such a man. But he refused all offers to join the exclusive parlours and groups of the city.

People gossiped about him nevertheless, calling him a merchant when he made money, ambitious when he distributed his wealth, an adventurer when he refused honors and a brute when he refused the advances of the fashionable. But in 1820, the king appointed him Mayor again and the principal citizens as well as the people in the streets pleaded with him to accept. He yielded finally and what brought about this change of mind the most, was the angry exclamation from a poor, old woman.

"A good mayor is a good thing," she shouted at him angrily. "Are you afraid of the good you can do?"

This was the third step in Father Madeleine's ascent. From Father he became Monsieur Madeleine, and finally Monsieur the Mayor. He remained as simple as before. He had grey hair, a serious eye, the brown complexion of a laborer and the countenance of a philosopher. He wore a hat with a wide brim and a long coat of coarse cloth. He lived the life of a recluse after fulfilling his duties of mayor. He smiled to avoid talking and donated to avoid smiling.

He took pleasure in walking the fields alone. He loved books, which were his only friends. His language became more polished, gentle and clearer every year.

Even though he wasn't young, he possessed great strength. He was reported picking up a fallen horse, pushing a stalled wheel and seizing a loose bull by the horns. His pockets were full of money when he went out and empty when he returned. He did good deeds as secretly as bad ones are done, breaking into houses and depositing a gold coin on the table. Rumors did the rounds that he was a dark, mysterious man and his room was a grotto like cell full of death's heads and cross-bones. The naughtier of the elegant ladies of M____ visited him and requested Monsieur Mayor to show them his room. They were well punished for their curiosity as he obliged with a smile. It was a room filled up with ugly mahogany furniture and shilling paper covering the walls. Only

two antique, silver candlesticks stood on the mantle. But rumors still went that the mayor's chamber was a hermit's cave, a tomb. Whispers also suggested that he had enormous sums deposited with the Lafitte banking house, to the tune of two or three millions. But in reality, that sum had dwindled down to six hundred and forty thousand francs.

In 1821, Monsieur Myriel, Bishop of D___ passed away and Monsieur Madeleine mourned by dressing in black. This became the talk of the town. It was assumed that he was related to the Bishop. But he denied this when questioned, saying that he was a servant in the Bishop's family when young. It was also observed that the mayor would send for any young Savoyard who was tramping about, ask him his name and give him money. Soon, many Savoyards started visiting the place.

Chapter Seven

Javert

The slanders slowly reduced to satire and then to wit and then vanished completely one day. People arrived from thirty miles away to consult Monsieur Madeleine because he prevented lawsuits, settled differences and reconciled enemies. But only one man seemed indifferent to Monsieur Madeleine, and his name was Javert. This tall man followed Madeleine with his eyes whenever he saw him. He would shake his head with a grimace that might be read as: "I am sure I have seen that man somewhere before."

This inspector of police named Javert was not there on the day that Madeleine arrived

in town. Javert enjoyed the protection of Monsieur Chabouillet, the secretary of the Minister of State, Count Angles, the then prefect of police at Paris. Javert arrived at M___ only after Father Madeleine had become Monsieur Madeleine. Inspector Javert was a terror to all that were related to the criminal world and Monsieur Madeleine noticed his suspicious eye, but he chose to ignore it. He treated Javert just as he treated everyone else, with ease and kindness. But one day, something rather strange happened.

Monsieur Madeleine was walking in an alley, when he heard a shout for help. An old man named Father Fauchelevent had fallen under his cart, when his horse was thrown down. This man was one of the sworn enemies of Monsieur Madeleine. His business had gone on the decline after Madeleine had prospered and this had filled him with jealousy and bitterness. He had done all he could to harm Madeleine.

Soon, Fauchelevent had become bankrupt and was forced to work as a carman for a living. Even now the old man had been unlucky, as he had fallen in such a manner, that his whole weight rested on his chest and he was caught between the wheels. All efforts to pull him out had been in vain and one false push would crush him. The only way to rescue him would be to raise the wagon from beneath. Javert, who was present, sent for a jack.

Monsieur Madeleine arrived and the crowd fell back with respect. "We cannot wait for a quarter of an hour," he exclaimed, after learning that the jack would take that much time to arrive. The wagon was sinking and Madeleine offered five and then ten Louis to anyone who would crawl under the wagon and lift it with his back. No one moved. "Twenty louis!" Madeleine cried, but still no one moved.

"They lack the strength and not the willingness," Javert declared. "I know only one man who is capable of such a feat, Monsieur Madeleine. He was a convict in the galleys at Toulon!"

Madeleine became pale.

"I am dying! Help me!" Fauchelevent screamed suddenly. Madeleine looked around for an instant and then was under the cart in a flash. For a moment, there was total silence. Then, the cart rose slowly. "Help! Quickly!" Madeleine cried and everyone rushed to help him. The courage of one man had fueled strength in others. Old Fauchelevent was saved as the cart was lifted by twenty arms. Fauchelevent had broken his knee-pan in the fall. Father Madeleine had carried him to his factory infirmary that was attended by two sisters of charity. The next morning, the old man discovered a thousand franc bill beside his bed, with a note from Madeleine stating that he had purchased his horse and cart. The cart was broken and the horse, dead! With Monsieur

Mayor Monsieur Madeleine

Madeleine's recommendation, Fauchelevent found a gardener's job at a convent.

No one remembered Fantine when she returned home. She presented herself at Madeleine's factory and found employment there to start earning her living. One morning, Javert paid Monsieur Madeleine a visit in his office. Javert stated that he had committed a criminal act and should be dismissed from service immediately. "Monsieur Mayor, six weeks ago, I was angry and denounced you to the Prefecture of Police at Paris."

It was a rarity for Monsieur Madeleine to laugh but he did so now.

"As a former convict," Javert added, and the mayor became livid. "I believed in it as the signs were there; a resemblance, your enormous strength, skill as a marksman, your dragging leg. I thought you were Jean Valjean."

"What? How do you pronounce that name?"

"Jean Valjean, a convict I saw twenty years ago when I was adjutant of the galley guard at

Toulon. The man robbed a bishop after leaving the galleys and robbed a small Savoyard on the highway. His whereabouts have been unknown for eight years. But now, the real Jean Valjean has been found."

"Ah," Monsieur Madeleine stated as the paper fell from his hands. "A simple and poor man called Father Champmathieu living in the country. He was arrested for stealing cider apples and imprisoned at Arras. A former convict named Brevet identified Champmathieu as Jean Valjean. Champmathieu denied it but the two other convicts for life who had seen him, identified him as well."

Inspector Javert requested that he be dismissed from service for having unjustly suspected his superior. "You are worthy of promotion and not dismissal," the mayor insisted. But Javert insisted that he be dismissed and exited with a bow.

Chapter Eight

The Champmathieu Affair

The reader must have realized that Monsieur Madeleine was none other than Jean Valjean. His objective to become a good and honest man had been achieved. But had he become a robber again? He reflected. Had he not robbed another man of his very existence, life, peace and place in the world? He must go to Arras to deliver the wrong Jean Valjean and denounce the right one. He wrote a letter to his banker, sealed it and put it in his pocket. Then, he left.

The Judge of the Royal Court of Douai was holding the trial and when he learnt that Monsieur Madeleine wanted to witness

the trial, he immediately ordered that he be brought in. The officer brought the respects of the judge to the mayor and escorted him to the counsel chamber. All he had to do was open the door, to find himself behind the judge's chair in the court room. Madeleine entered the court room slowly.

No one in the multitude paid any attention to him. Their eyes were fixed on the prisoner in the witness box. Madeleine thought he saw himself, only older. The man was similar in appearance. The mayor was finally noticed. The judge greeted him with a bow and so did the prosecuting attorney. He sank into a chair and realized that the trial had been in progress for three hours. But the prisoner still denied the charges.

The time had arrived to close the case. The judge summoned the convicts Brevet, Chenildieu and Cochepaille, to identify Jean Valjean. All three insisted that the man who

claimed to be Champmathieu was in fact, Jean Valjean. Suddenly, a voice called out the three convicts by name and everyone turned towards the source of this voice.

"Monsieur Madeleine!" they exclaimed in unison.

"Do you not recognize me?" the mayor stated, approaching the three convicts who shook their heads in denial.

"Gentlemen of the jury, release the accused," the mayor ordered. "Your honor, order my arrest. I am Jean Valjean!"

No one in the court stirred. The sympathetic judge and prosecuting attorney cnquired if there was a physician in court.

"I thank you but I am not mad," the mayor stated. He recounted as to how Brevet had checkered, knit suspenders in the galleys. A surprised Brevet looked at him wildly from head to toe. He recalled Cochepaille's tattoo on his left arm as the date the emperor landed at Cannes.

MARCH 1st
1815

He ordered the convict to roll up his sleeve. *March 1st, 1815* was revealed in blue letters.

"You see! I am Jean Valjean," the mayor declared.

Everyone forgot what they were supposed to do; the judge forgot he was supposed to preside, the prosecuting attorney forgot he was supposed to prosecute and the counsel for the defense forgot to defend. It was evident that this man was Jean Valjean but no one was willing to make a move. Jean Valjean announced that he was leaving as he was not being arrested. He could be arrested whenever they wanted to. An hour later, Champmathieu was released and he went his way, thinking all men were mad!

Chapter Nine

Fantine's Death

Fantine had a feverish and sleepless night but was happy when she slept at daybreak. Sister Simplice who attended to her, was paid a visit by M. Madeleine. She informed him that Fantine's health had improved once she learnt that the mayor had gone to fetch her child.

"Will not Monsieur Mayor not fetch her child?" she asked fearfully.

"Certainly, but two or three days are needed."

The sister objected when the mayor wanted to see Fantine as she would be heartbroken not to see her child with him. But he insisted that he must see her as he might not have much

time left. Fantine was sleeping when the mayor entered her room but she opened her eyes and enquired with a smile, "And Cosette?"

Thankfully, the physician came to the mayor's aid as Fantine talked a lot, breaking into sporadic coughing fits. The mayor assured Fantine that he would fetch her child for her, but her eyes seemed to be arrested by someone at the door. It was Javert! Fantine saw Javert take the mayor by the collar. "Come along, Jean Valjean!" he ordered.

"Javert," Jean Valjean began, without attempting to loosen Javert's grip.

"Call me Monsieur the Inspector!" Javert insisted.

"I have a request. Give me three days to go for the child of this unhappy woman," Jean Valjean stated. "I will pay whatever's necessary. You can accompany me if you want."

"Do you think I'm so stupid?" Javert laughed. "You ask for three days to escape?"

"My child!" Fantine exclaimed. "She is not here then? I want my Cosette, Monsieur the Mayor."

"There's no mayor," Javert declared. "There is a robber and a convict here called Jean Valjean and I have got him now!"

Fantine gasped and sank back into her pillow. Her head struck the head of the bed, her mouth gaped and her eyes were open and glazed. Fantine was dead!

Jean Valjean loosened Javert's hand as if it was a child's hand. "You have killed this woman!" he stated.

"Have done with this!" Javert said furiously. "Save your sermons as I'm not here to listen to them. The guard is below. Come along or be handcuffed!"

Jean Valjean wrenched out the rickety head bar from a dilapidated old iron bed in a corner of the room. He stared at Javert who recoiled towards the door in fear.

"I advise you not to disturb me now," he said softly. Javert trembled but did not call the guard.

He reclined against the door and watched Jean Valjean, who arranged Fantine's head carefully on the pillow. Fastening the string of her night-dress and replacing her hair beneath her cap, he closed her eyes. Fantine's face glowed. Death is the entrance to the great light! Jean Valjean kissed Fantine's hand. Then he rose and addressed Javert, "Now, I am at your disposal!"

Jean Valjean was put in the city prison and this arrest caused a sensation throughout town. Strangely, almost everyone with the exception of three or four people abandoned him upon learning that he was a galley slave. The old portress who was his servant was one of them and she was stunned to see her master enter the house through the window. He had escaped from prison and ordered her to fetch Sister Simplice. He gave her a letter that instructed the Cure to take charge of whatever he had left there. The expenses of his trial and Fantine's burial were to be taken from his money. The remainder should be given to the poor.

There was a loud noise heard on the staircase. When Javert entered the room despite the protests of the old portress that no one had come here, he discovered the sister praying in the room. Javert knew that the sister had never lied in her life. He asked her if she was alone in the room.

"Yes," she lied. He asked her if she had seen Jean Valjean and the nun lied again. Two lies in succession from someone who had never lied.

"Your pardon," Javert bowed respectfully, and withdrew. He did not even notice the smoking candle that had just been extinguished on the table.

An hour later, a man walked speedily in the dark towards Paris. The man was Jean Valjean. A few wagoners testified later that he was carrying a bundle and was dressed in a blouse. How had he got this blouse? An old artisan had died in his infirmary a few days ago, leaving behind only his blouse. It could be that one.

ORION

Chapter Ten

Cosette

Jean Valjean had been retaken in Paris after four days and sent back to the galleys at Toulon. Number 24601 now became Number 9430. It was 1823, and the same year, the ship Orion arrived at the port of Toulon to repair its damages. From morning to night, the port was full of people who came to gaze at this magnificent ship. One morning, these idlers witnessed an accident. The crew was busy furling sail when the topman lost his balance and hung suspended from the man-ropes. He hung from there, swinging like a pendulum over the sea below. To rescue him was a frightful

risk, and no sailor dared attempt it. The sailor tried in vain to ascend and each movement made him weaker. It seemed he would be flung to his death in the sea, when a man was spotted climbing up like a wildcat.

The man was a convict, as his red dress indicated and his green cap showed that he was a convict for life. A gust of wind blew away his cap, to reveal his white head. He was not a young man. But he was upon the yard in a flash and appeared to measure it with his glance. The crowd drew its breath as he ran along the yard. He reached the extreme tip and fastened an end of the rope he was carrying, letting the other end hang at full length. He descended using this rope and the terror doubled as two men were hanging precariously with the rope now.

The convict reached the seaman to secure him firmly to the rope he held. He started his ascent to the yard, hauling the sailor after him. He reached the yard, carrying the sailor in his

arms to walk along the yard to reach the round-top where he deposited the sailor to the hands of his mates. The convict now started descending immediately to return to his work. But the crowd cried in unison as he slipped and fell into the sea.

The fall was perilous, as the convict fell between the Orion and the frigate *Algesiras,* anchored beside it. It was feared he would be drawn under one ship. Four men jumped into a boat immediately but the convict did not resurface. The search continued till the night, but the dead body was not found. The *Toulon Journal* published the following lines the next morning: - *"November 17, 1823. Yesterday, a convict at work on the Orion, fell into the sea after rescuing a sailor and was drowned. His body has not been discovered, and the man was registered by the number 9430, going by the name Jean Valjean."*

But Jean Valjean was not dead! He had thrown himself into the sea and had not died. He was free from his irons and had

swam underwater, to reach a boat fastened to an anchored ship. He hid himself in this boat till evening and took to the water again at night. He reached land near Cape Brun and finally reached Paris.

The first thing he did after reaching Paris, was to purchase a morning dress for a seven year old girl. Then, he went to Montfermeil and rescued Cosette from the clutches of the Thenardiers and returned to Paris. He stopped before the old Gorbeau house that seemed small as a cottage but was as wide as a cathedral. Almost the whole house was hidden and only a door and a window could be seen.

Cosette slept on, even though it was broad daylight. She was woken up by the sound of a carrier wagon that shook the old building. "Yes madame!" Cosette exclaimed, "Here I am. Where is my broom?" "Good morning, Monsieur," Cosette said, when she spotted Jean Valjean's smiling face. Children accept

happiness with quick familiarity, as they are naturally, happiness and joy. Cosette felt a sense of freedom even in her horrible surroundings.

"Must I sweep?" she asked.

"Play!" Jean Valjean replied. Cosette did not bother to think too much about it but she was very happy with her new doll and new friend.

For twenty-five years Jean Valjean had been alone in the world. He had never loved anything. Never had he been a father, lover, friend or husband. Cosette had moved his heart and there was a strong bond between this fifty-five year old man and this eight year old girl. Cosette could not recollect her mother as she was very small when she had left her. Everybody else had mistreated her and when she received kindness and love for the first time, she naturally loved back in return.

The house had several rooms but there was only one more inhabitant. An old woman lived in one room and served as Jean Valjean's maid. Jean Valjean started teaching Cosette how to

read and spell. She called him *Father* and Jean Valjean wanted to live till he was old now as he had a purpose to do so; a child who loved him. Jean Valjean was no less weak than Cosette. Who knows, he might have fallen back to evil ways again? Thanks to the arrival of love, he became strong again. Just like he was Cosette's support, she gave him strength to remain virtuous.

Jean Valjean was prudent enough to venture out in the day. He would take a walk for a couple of hours in the night sometimes alone, and sometimes with Cosette. He was perceived as a beggar on the street with kind-hearted dames handing him a penny. He would accept and quietly slip the penny in a beggar's hands when no one was looking. He became known as *the beggar who gave alms.* The old landlady of the old Gorbeau House had a curious nature and a keen sense of observation and she watched Jean Valjean closely, without arousing his suspicion. She had questioned Cosette but learnt nothing

except that she was from Montfermeil. The old lady spied on Jean Valjean and was frightened when she saw him take out a bank bill of a thousand francs from his coat. It was only the second or third one she had seen in her life. Later, Jean Valjean asked her to get the bill changed for him, stating it was the half-yearly interest on his property that he had received. "Where?" thought the old woman, as he did not go out till six o' clock and the government treasury was closed then. But she changed the note for him.

One day, Jean Valjean encountered a beggar whose face appeared very familiar. But he could not admit to himself that he had seen the face of Javert.

One morning, Jean Valjean spotted a stranger in the house. From the back, it was the unmistakable frame of Inspector Javert. He questioned the old lady, who informed him that a new lodger had arrived at the house. Jean Valjean collected Cosette as they had to escape immediately.

As Jean Valjean looked at the corner of the street, he saw eight soldiers led by Javert, marching in a platoon. There was no doubt who they were searching for. Jean Valjean looked at the wall. It was the only means of escape. He knew how to scale it but Cosette didn't. He did not possess a rope as well. This was an extreme situation and sometimes these kinds of situations blind us and sometimes they illuminate us. Jean Valjean's eyes fell on a lamp-post and he was struck by an idea. These street lights were lowered or raised by a rope traversing the street from end to end. In an instant, Jean Valjean crossed the street, used his knife to spring the bolt of the small box and returned with his precious rope. He took off his cravat, passing it around Cosette's body carefully. Then, he tied the cravat to an end of the rope via a knot that seamen call a swallow knot. Taking the other end of the rope in his teeth, he flung his shoes

and stockings over the wall. Then he scaled the wall like a monkey and ordered a stunned Cosette to put her back against the wall. She obeyed and was lifted slowly off the ground to the top of the wall. Jean Valjean put her on his back lay down flat and crawled to the far corner, where there was a building near a lime-tree. The top of this building sloped down gently to the lime-tree and it was easier to descend from here with Cosette.

Jean Valjean slid down the roof, keeping a grip on Cosette and reached the lime-tree, to jump onto the ground. They found themselves in a large garden. It was a dilapidated building with a few dismantled rooms. Jean Valjean and Cosette sought refuge in a small shed, as they heard a terrible racket as the soldiers searched for them. Then, there was calm and this was broken by a beautiful celestial hymn that emerged from the gloomy building opposite the darkness. It was almost like the sound of

angels after the demons had left. Cosette and Jean Valjean fell on their knees in prayer. The chant stopped and there was silence again.

It was cold and Jean Valjean covered Cosette with his coat. The child went off to sleep on a stone. Suddenly, Jean Valjean heard a noise and spotted a man in the garden with a bell. He walked slowly with a limp, on the melon patch. Jean Valjean gathered Cosette and moved to a dark corner of the shed. Suddenly, he discovered that Cosette's hands were icy. He shook her but she did not wake. "Is she dead?" he exclaimed, with a shudder. Jean Valjean approached the man in the garden. "A hundred francs, if you give me shelter tonight," he exclaimed. "Why, it's Father Madeleine!" the man exclaimed and Jean Valjean was stunned. He had expected anything but this. The man was old, bent and lame, and Jean Valjean couldn't recognize him. "How did you come here, Father Madeleine?" the man enquired. "Who are you? What is this house?" Jean Valjean asked.

"You are the one who got me here. You saved my life!" the old man exclaimed. "Don't you remember? This is the convent of the Petit Picpus."

It was then that Jean Valjean recognized old Fauchelevent and asked him for his help. Fauchelevent followed Jean Valjean like a dog follows his master. They fetched Cosette and half an hour later, rosy again before a good fire, she was asleep on the old gardener's bed. Jean Valjean and Fauchelevent threw themselves upon a bundle of straw each after having a glass of wine and a piece of cheese, as the only bed was occupied by Cosette. But neither man slept while Jean Valjean confessed that he had to stay there now. He knew that this was the only place where he could be safe with Cosette. Fauchelevent thought a lot about this, as no man other than him was officially allowed to enter the convent. It was a punishable offence and Fauchelevent arrived at a difficult decision; he would devote

himself to Monsieur Madeleine. Fauchelevent took Jean Valjean and Cosette to the prioress and introduced them as his brother Ultimus and his granddaughter. The prioress agreed to recruit Jean Valjean as an assistant-gardener and also enrolled Cosette as a charity pupil in the school building. A pleasant life began again for Jean Valjean as he made himself busy in the garden. His early life as a pruner made him a good worker in the garden and he made the orchard trees bear excellent fruit. Cosette was permitted to spend an hour with him every day. The sisters were melancholy and as he was kind, Cosette worshipped him. For Jean Valjean, it was Paradise when Cosette arrived and he sadly looked at her room when she left. Jean Valjean's heart melted with gratitude at this new life and he loved her more and more. Many years passed by and Cosette grew up.

Chapter Eleven

Marius

M. Gillenormand was a strange old man in 1831. He was a genuine bourgeois of the eighteenth century, and a rare specimen. He walked erect, drank hard, had clear vision, slept and snored, and spoke loudly even in his ninetieth year. His unmarried daughter was fifty years old and he treated her as an eight year old.

The two daughters of M. Gillenormand were born ten years apart. They did not resemble each other both in character and countenance. The younger was cheerful and fond of flowers, poetry and music. She had the wings of an angel while her elder sister had those of a goose. The younger did manage to marry the man of her dreams but died. The elder, though a spinster, was still alive. She was so insignificant that no one outside the immediate family knew her real name. She was addressed as *Mademoiselle Gillenormand the elder.*

She was as modest as an English Miss and age had increased this pitiless modesty. The title *Prude* seemed to fit her perfectly and she spent hours in an old-fashioned Jesuit altar in a chapel, praying her heart out. She kept her father's house and in this house of old man and old maid, there was a little boy- a child, as well. He was always shaking and trembling before M. Gillenormand who always spoke to him sternly but he idolized him. This child was his grandson.

Many walled compartments existed near the bridge that bordered the left bank of the Seine river. There were many charming flower enclosures here. A man of about fifty lived in the smallest of these houses with a woman who waited upon him. Gardening was his occupation and the square of earth which was his garden was famous for the beauty of its flowers. People who had read the military memoirs, biographies and bulletins would be well versed with the name George Pontmercy. As a young man, he was a soldier in the regiment of Saintonage. This regiment was in the Army of the Rhine when the revolution had broken out. Pontmercy had displayed extraordinary bravery at battle many times, receiving the Cross from the Emperor. Apart from the Legion of Honour, he also received the rank of Colonel, and the title of a Baron. After Waterloo, Pontmercy was badly injured and was put on half pay.

He had married Mademoiselle Gillenormand against the wishes of her father. Madame Pontmercy died in 1815, leaving behind a child. The grandfather then wanted custody of this

child, telling Pontmercy that he would disinherit the child otherwise. The father yielded for his son's sake, making the ultimate sacrifice as he was told that if he met his son, the latter would be immediately disinherited. Not able to love his son, he set about loving flowers instead. Pontmercy gave up everything and hired the smallest house in Vernon, doing what we have already described.

The child named Marius, knew that he had a father but nothing else. He was not allowed to meet his father but when he grew up, he heard all that was whispered about his father in his grandfather's society. He felt only shame and disgust towards his father. Pontmercy escaped to Paris sometimes but observed his son as he went to church, concealed behind a pillar.

The cure of Vernon, Abbe Mabeuf and the warden, had spotted this man with a scar on his cheek behind the pillar, weeping like a woman. One day, on a visit to Vernon, the warden saw the man again. He spoke of it to the cure and the two paid Pontmercy a visit. This visit led to others and the old priest and the old soldier became close friends. Both were devoted men; one to his country in heaven and the other to his country on earth. The priest ensured now that father and son started writing letters to each other twice a year.

In 1827, Marius turned eighteen and his grandfather approached him with a letter in his hand. "You will set out tomorrow for Vernon to see your father," he ordered. Marius shuddered as nothing was more surprising or disagreeable than meeting his father. It was clear to him that his father did not love him, having abandoned him. "He is sick, and is asking for you," his grandfather added.

Marius arrived at Vernon at dusk and sought out the house of Monsieur Pontmercy. He rang the bell and the door was opened by a woman holding a small lamp.

"Mosnieur Pontmercy?" Marius enquired, but the woman was silent.

"I am his son. He is expecting me."

"He expects you no more," the woman replied, in tears. She pointed to the door of a low room and Marius entered. He saw three men in the room; a priest prayed, a physician stood and the third man lay on the floor, stripped to his shirt.

Three days ago, the colonel had been attacked with brain fever. He had written to Monsieur Gillenormand to send his son and when Marius had not arrived, he jumped out of the bed to go and meet his son. He fell on the floor of the hall and had just breathed his last. The doctor and the son, both had come too late! Marius stared at his dead father, saw the lines of heroism on his body in the form of brown lined saber-cuts and red star bullet holes and the gigantic scar on his face. Yet, Marius was unmoved, not having known his father. The colonel had left nothing for Marius, except a letter.

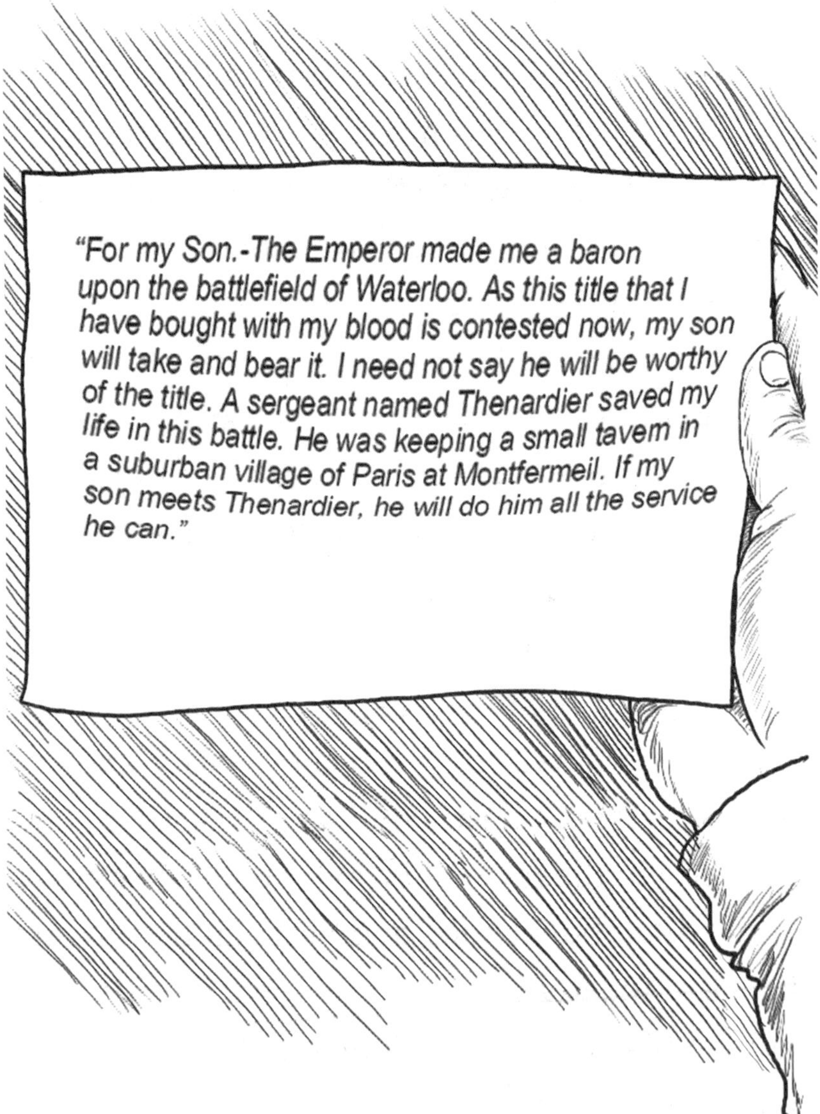
"For my Son.-The Emperor made me a baron upon the battlefield of Waterloo. As this title that I have bought with my blood is contested now, my son will take and bear it. I need not say he will be worthy of the title. A sergeant named Thenardier saved my life in this battle. He was keeping a small tavem in a suburban village of Paris at Montfermeil. If my son meets Thenardier, he will do him all the service he can."

"For my Son.-The Emperor made me a baron upon the battlefield of Waterloo. As this title that I have bought with my blood is contested now, my son will take and bear it. I need not say he will be worthy of the title. A sergeant named Thenardier saved my life in this battle. He was keeping a small tavern in a suburban village of Paris at Montfermeil. If my son meets Thenardier, he will do him all the service he can."

Marius took the letter more as respect for the dead rather than a sense of duty. No trace remained of the colonel. His sword and uniform were sold to a second hand dealer by Monsieur Gillenormand. The neighbours stripped the garden and took the rare flowers as the other ones died in neglect. Marius returned to Paris after the burial. The colonel was buried in two days and forgotten in three.

One day, as Marius attended mass, the priest named Mabeuf came and introduced himself to him. Earlier, the priest had asked Marius to remove himself from behind a pillar when he saw him kneeling there.

"Let me explain my impertinence. This is the place of a poor, brave and loving father," he said to Marius. "This man came here to catch a glimpse of his son when he came to mass. He had no other way of seeing his son. Family arrangements prevented him from doing so and he wept when he saw his child as he literally worshipped him. This man's father-in-law threatened to disinherit the child if he saw him and the father sacrificed himself so that his son would be rich and happy one day. Bless me! A man is not a monster if he has been to Waterloo and a father cannot be separated from his child for that. He was one of Bonaparte's colonels, with a handsome sabre cut and is now dead, I believe. He lived at Vernon, and his name is…"

"Pontmercy," a pale Marius exclaimed.

"Yes. Did you know him?"

"He was my father!"

"Ah, you are the child!" the priest exclaimed. "Well, poor child. You can say that you had a father who loved you more than anything else."

The next day Marius said to his grandfather, "We have arranged a hunting party with a few friends. Will you allow me to be absent for three days?"

"Take four. Go amuse yourself," his grandfather replied, whispering with a wink to his daughter, "Some love affair!"

Marius returned to Paris after a three-day absence, heading straight for the law school library. He asked for a file of the *Moniteur* and read all the histories of the republic and the Empire. Marius slowly started admiring his father. After he was through, he ordered a hundred cards from an engraver that said: *Baron Marius Pontmercy.*

Marius was once away to Montfermeil for four days in search of Thenardier. He couldn't find the man but this act worried his aunt and

grandfather, the latter sure that he was going astray. His Aunt Gillenormand, employed the services of her grand-nephew Theodule, who was a lancer in the garrison to keep an eye on Marius. He was going to his new station and had stopped to pay his aunt a visit. He was travelling in the same diligence as Marius and would get off at Vernon to take the branch for Gaillon. Mademoiselle Gillenormand asked Theodule to see the woman Marius was seeing, and write to them about her. Marius and Theodule boarded the diligence, but the latter forgot all about his duty and fell asleep promptly. He woke up only at daybreak, when the driver shouted for passengers of Vernon to disembark. He wondered about Marius then, and saw him purchase flowers from a peasant girl. This interested Theodule, and he followed Marius, who walked towards the church.

"Is he in love?" Theodule thought.

Marius did not enter the church but went behind the building. "Let me see the lass now," Theodule exclaimed and followed. He advanced on tiptoe towards the corner Marius had taken and peeped. He was stunned! Marius knelt on the ground, upon a grave, his face hidden in his hands. He had scattered his flowers all over the grave. The black wooden cross displayed the white letters: COLONEL BARON PONTMERCY. He heard Marius sobbing. The lass was a tomb!

When Marius returned to the house, his grandfather ran up as fast as he could to meet him and solve this mystery. But Marius had left his room and his grandfather fetched the little box and Marius's coat he found on his bed, to display to his eldest daughter. "We shall discover what the mystery is," he declared and opened the box to find a piece of paper.

"It's a love letter!" the old man exclaimed.

"Ah! Let us read it," the aunt exclaimed.

They read the letter that was Marius's father's letter to him. Both father and daughter were shocked and just then a package fell from Marius's coat pocket. In it, were the hundred cards that read: *Baron Marius Pontmercy.* Marius walked in a few minutes later and the old man confronted Marius, who defended his father as an honorable and brave man.

"All who served B-u-o-naparte were bandits and traitors," the old man thundered. "They betrayed the legitimate king and were cowards who ran from the Prussians and English at Waterloo!"

Marius was enraged now, as it was beyond him to insult his grandfather. At the same time, he had to avenge his father.

"Down with the Bourbons and the great hog Louis XVIII!" he thundered. The fact that Louis XVIII had been dead for four years did not matter to him. The old man turned whiter than his hair at this insult.

"A baron like you and a bourgeois cannot live under the same roof," he cried angrily. "Be off!"

So, Marius left the house and the old man instructed his daughter to send him sixty pistoles every six months and never mention Marius to him again. Marius left the house with thirty francs, his watch and a few clothes in a carpet bag. Hiring a cabriolet, he headed towards the Latin Quarter. Life became horrible for Marius, as he endured days without bread, nights without sleep and evenings without a candle. There was a hearth without a fire, a future without hope and clothes that made young girls laugh. Marius swallowed insults like the jibes of neighbours and the insolence of the landlord among other things. He purchased a mutton cutlet for six or seven sous, cooked it himself and lived on it for three days. The first day he ate the meat, the second day, the fat and on the third day, he gnawed the bone. Marius

always sent back the sixty pistoles sent by his aunt, stating he didn't need anything.

Marius continued being dressed in black to mourn his dead father. But one day, his coat gave away and his trousers were going to. Courfeyrac, to whom he had done some favors, gave him an old coat. For thirty sous, Marius had it repaired to resemble a new one. As this coat was green, Marius went outdoors only at night, as it made the green coat black. He desired to be in mourning always and clothed himself with night. Despite these troubles, Marius obtained admission to the bar. He occupied Courfeyrac's room and a few law books here, supported by old novels sufficed to serve as the required library as per the rules. Through a letter, Marius politely informed his grandfather that he had become a lawyer. M. Gillenormand read the letter with trembling hands, tore it up and threw it in the basket.

Just like everything else, misery becomes endurable too. By sheer hard work and

determination, Marius began to earn seven hundred francs a year. Thanks to Courfeyrac, Marius learned German and English and found a place in the literary department of a publishing house owned by Courfeyrac's friend. Marius lived in a lousy little room at the Gorbeau tenement, paying an annual rent of thirty francs. There was no fireplace, no cabinet and even the furniture was his own. He paid three francs to the old woman who swept his room and brought him a little warm water, a fresh egg and a penny loaf of bread every morning. This was his breakfast that cost two to four sous. He dined at six in the evening at Rousseau's, at Rue Saint Jacques. He ate a sixpenny plate of meat, a threepenny plate of vegetables and a threepenny dessert and as much bread as he could for three sous. He drank water in place of wine. He tipped a sou to the waiter and had dinner for sixteen sous. So, his food cost him twenty sous a day, amounting to

three hundred sixty five francs a year. Adding thirty francs for lodging, thirty-six francs paid to the old woman and other expenses, Marius was fed, lodged and waited upon for four hundred and fifty francs.

His clothes cost him a hundred francs, his linen fifty francs and his washing fifty more. Total expenses were six hundred and fifty francs and he saved fifty francs. He was rich! Marius had two black suits; an old one for everyday wear and a new one for special occasions. He had only three shirts, one he had on, the second in his drawer and the third at the washerwoman's. Hard years had been faced by Marius to reach this stage and he had never given up for a single day. He had never got into debt and rather than borrow, he preferred not to eat. To find Thenardier, the man who had saved his father's life was also foremost on Marius's mind.

Three years after leaving his grandfather, Marius turned twenty years old. They did not

attempt to reconcile and Marius assumed that the old man had never loved him. But Marius was deceived; there are fathers who do not love their children but there is no grandfather who does not adore his grandson. M. Gillenormand worshipped Marius.

One day, the old woman who waited upon Marius told him that his neighbours, the wretched Jondrette family, were to be turned into the street for not paying their rent.

"How much?"

"Twenty francs," the old woman replied. "They owe for two terms."

Marius had thirty francs in reserve in his drawer.

"Here," he said to the old woman. "Here are twenty-five francs. Pay for these poor people and give them five francs. Do not tell them that it is from me."

Chapter Twelve

Marius Falls in Love

Marius was now a handsome man and even when he was poor, girls turned when he passed. He would flee as he thought they looked at his old clothes or laughed at his poverty. So, Marius shied away from all women. For more than a year, Marius had spotted an old man and a young girl sitting together in a retired walk of the Luxembourg. The man was about sixty, serious and sad but with a kind expression on his face. The girl was about fourteen, ugly but had fine eyes. Marius had a mechanical habit of taking a walk here and he always found them seated at the same place.

The next year, Marius stopped going to this place for a walk and went there after a gap of six months. He spotted the same pair again but was astonished to see that the girl had turned into a beautiful creature. She had a smile like sunshine and a voice like music. One day, nature was at its beautiful best as Marius took his walk and as he passed by the young girl, their eyes met and locked briefly. She looked down and he continued on his way.

The next day, Marius dressed in his best clothes and walked slower than usual. He passed the girl and thought she bent to take a look at him. He dared not look but returned, although he could not approach her seat again. Instead, he sat down and cast sidelong glances from time to time. After fifteen minutes, he went home, forgetting to go for dinner. He was eating a piece of bread, when he realized it was too late to go for dinner. Marius went to bed after he brushed and folded his coat carefully.

U.F.

Marius kept going to the Luxembourg, and on one of the last days of the second week, the girl held his father's arm, and walked by Marius. She looked at him sweetly and thoughtfully and that made his heart tremble. Marius was desperately in love! It seemed that she was reproaching him not to have approached him and so, she had had to do the needful. An entire month passed like this and nothing could keep Marius away at this hour. He became bolder and sat nearer to where the girl sat. One day, Marius found a white handkerchief on the seat where the girl sat. It was marked U.F. and he immediately assumed that the girl's name was Ursula. Marius kissed the handkerchief, inhaled its perfume and even slept with it on his lips. Little did Marius know that the handkerchief belonged to the old gentleman, who had simply let it fall from his pocket.

Marius followed Ursula to discover that she lived in Rue de 1'Ouest, in a modest three-

story house. The next day, the old man saw Marius outside their house and looked at him steadily. The next day, they did not come at the Luxembourg. A week passed by but they still did not come and Marius was shocked when he made enquiries of the porter in the house. The old man and his daughter had moved.

Summer passed, then autumn and winter arrived. But there was no sign of the young girl and the old man in Luxembourg. Marius was heartbroken and it seemed all was over for him. Marius lived in anguish, till one day, in one of the streets of the Boulevard des Invalides, he saw a man who appeared to be a laborer. Marius's attention was arrested by the old man's white hair under his cap and he seemed to recognize the old man at the Luxembourg. But what surprised Marius was the working man's clothes on the old man.

One day, Marius was paid a visit by Jondrette's eldest daughter. She carried a letter for Marius, in which her father thanked Marius for his kindness for paying their rent. He also stated that they had been without bread for two days, four people and that his wife was sick. He requested Marius's help who gave his daughter five francs, resisting her flirtatious advances. On her way out, the girl spotted a dry crust of bread lying in the dust and ate it up in a flash.

Marius reproached himself now for being insensitive enough not to see the suffering of his neighbours. He could hear them through the thin walls that separated them and they did seem to be depraved, corrupt, vile and hateful. There is a point where the infamous and the unfortunate are associated and confounded in a single, fatal word –

Les Misérables!

But whose fault is it? Should it not be that when the fall is lowest that charity ought to be greatest? Marius reflected and suddenly noticed a triangular hole near the ceiling on that old wall of plaster, that separated the neighbours from him.

"Let us see what these people are," Marius decided, "and to what they are reduced."

He climbed up to the crevice and looked through it.

Marius saw the eldest daughter announce to her father that the old gentleman was coming. The father sprang up happily and ordered his wife to put out the fire. When the stunned woman did not stir, he threw water over the fire himself. Then, he ruined the chair seat by putting his foot through it. He ordered his younger girl to break a pane of glass. The girl cut her hand as she did so and wept.

"What stupid things are you doing?" the mother exclaimed. "She has cut herself!"

"I knew she would," the man stated and quickly bandaged the little girl's bleeding hand.

"Now, we can receive the philanthropist," he declared.

Soon, there was a knock on the door and the man opened it to welcome the old man and a young lady. Marius's heart stopped beating. It was She! The girl Marius loved entered with her old man and laid down a large package on the table.

"Monsieur, there are some new clothes, stockings and coverlids in this package," the old man declared.

"Thank you, our angelic benefactor," the man exclaimed. "Look, no bread, no fire. My only chair unseated! A broken window in this weather! My wife in bed, sick!"

"Poor woman!" the old man exclaimed.

"My child injured," Jondrette added, as the young woman went to comfort the child.

"Look, my beautiful young lady," Jondrette continued. "Her bleeding wrist caused by an accident working at a machine to earn six sous a day. It might be necessary to cut off her arm."

The little girl took this seriously and wailed. Jondrette had been watching the old man closely as if to recollect where he had seen him before. When he and his daughter were busy with his child, he rushed to his wife and whispered to her to take good notice of the old man. Then, he continued his lamentations, saying he owed four quarters a year that is sixty francs. He was lying of course, as four quarters amounted to forty and not sixty francs in the first place. The old man gave him five francs and promised to bring him the rest that evening. He also left behind his overcoat for Jondrette to wear.

Marius continued watching, as Jondrette stated that they needed two chairs. "I will get our neighbor's," his wife stated and Marius had enough time to hide under the bed, as she entered his room, grabbed the two chairs he owned and left. Marius took out his pistol and cocked it. Jondrette started at the sound and exclaimed, "Who is there?"

Marius held his breath and then, Jondrette laughed.

"What a fool I am! It's the partition cracking!"

As six o' clock struck, the old man had arrived. "Come in my benefactor, Monsieur Leblanc," Jondrette exclaimed. The old man laid four Louis upon the table.

"This is for your rent and other pressing needs," he said. "We shall see about the rest later."

"God bless you," Jondrette exclaimed.

Marius suddenly spotted a stranger enter and sit down on the bed. His arms were bare and tattooed and his face was stained black.

"Who is he?" M. Leblanc asked.

"He is a neighbour. Pay him no attention," Jondrette replied. A second man, similar to the first now entered and sat down on the bed. Jondrette displayed a painting to M. Leblanc that he wished to sell. Soon, there were four strangers in the room in total.

"Don't mind them," Jondrette stated. "They are just neighbours, faces blackened because of

work in charcoal. Look at this painting by a master. Tell me how much it's worth."

"This is a tavern sign worth three francs," M. Leblanc replied.

"I shall be satisfied with a thousand crowns. Do you have your pocket book with you?" Jondrette stated. M. Leblanc rose to his feet with his back to the wall, and looked around the room.

The little man called Jondrette now took a step towards M. Leblanc and thundered, "But my real question is, do you know me?"

The door of the garret was flung open suddenly and three men in blue blouses and black paper masks entered. The first carried an iron cudgel, and the second a butcher's pole-axe. The third held a huge key from some prison door. It appeared that Jondrette was waiting for these men as a rapid dialogue ensued between him and the man with the cudgel. Then, he turned towards M. Leblanc and laughed horribly.

"You don't recognize me, then?"

"No!"

"My name is not Fabantou, my name is not Jondrette, my name is Thenardier!" Jondrette shrieked like a wild beast, as he moved his face M. Leblanc. "Do you know me now?"

"No more than before," M. Leblanc replied calmly.

Marius trembled when he heard the name 'Thenardier' and had to support himself from falling. He knew the name well, as it was written on his father's will. Marius's father had stated that Thenardier had saved his life and that Marius was supposed to do all the good he could for Thenardier. But this man was a monster!! Marius was caught in two minds now. If he fired his pistol, M. Leblanc would be saved from Thenardier. But if he didn't, the old man would have to be sacrificed.

"Monsieur Philanthropist," Thenardier cried triumphantly. "Monsieur threadbare

millionaire! I have found you at last! You arrived at my inn eight years ago, on Christmas night, in 1823. Weren't you the man who took away Fantine's child from my house? You child stealer!"

"I do not know what you mean," the old man replied. "I am a poor man and not a millionaire. You are mistaking me for another man. But I see that you are nothing but a bandit!"

"Yes, you rich people call us so," Thenardier replied. "And you, perhaps, are not one? Do you have anything else to declare before we begin to dance with you?"

M. Leblanc was silent and Thenardier was so enraged and overconfident about the old man being outnumbered that he turned his back to him. M. Leblanc seized this opportunity and reached the window in a flash. He was halfway outside, when six strong hands of the 'chimney doctors' dragged him back inside with the Thenardiess clutching him by the hair. Marius

saw the old man about to be clubbed and his finger sought out the trigger of his pistol.

"Forgive me father!" he said, as he was about to shoot.

"Do him no harm!" Thenardier ordered his men and Marius decided not to shoot but wait to see what happened.

M. Leblanc put up a valiant fight but was outnumbered and tied up at the foot of the bed. Thenardier offered the old man a bargain. He wanted two hundred thousand francs. He untied the old man's hands and asked him to write a letter to his daughter for the money. Then, Thenardier dispatched his wife to the address with the letter. Only five bandits remained with Thenardier and his prisoner now. The Thenardiess returned after half an hour. "False address!" she declared.

"What did you hope for by giving a false address?" Thenardier asked his prisoner angrily.

"To gain time," the old man replied as he shook himself free from his bonds. The prisoner was just attached to the bed by one leg now. He hadn't stopped down to cut the chords on his left leg for fear of betraying himself. Before his captors could react, he had picked up a glowing chisel from the fireplace.

"You are pitiable," he declared. "But my life is not worth so long a defense. As to you thinking that you can make me write what I do not wish to write and speak what I do not wish to speak, here..."

He laid the glowing chisel on his right arm and the bandits shuddered at the hissing sound of burning flesh. Marius was horrified but the old man's expression barely changed as the red hot iron burned on his wound. There was no hatred on the old man's face when he said, "Wretches! Have no fear for me than I have for you."

Throwing the chisel out of the open window, the prisoner declared, "Do with me what you will."

The Cognes are Here

Hands seized him immediately and it was decided by husband and wife that the old man would be killed. Thenardier took out a knife from the drawer and Marius reacted. He saw a piece of paper on which it was written by the elder of the Thenardier girls that very morning: "THE COGNES ARE HERE."

Using his brains, Marius threw this paper inside the room through the crevice.

"What is that?" Thenardier asked as he advanced towards his prisoner with the knife. His wife handed him the letter.

"It's Eponine's handwriting!" he exclaimed. There was a horrible rush now as everybody wanted to escape first from the room.

"Let us draw lots who shall go out first," one of the bandits suggested.

"Would you like my hat?" a voice enquired from the door. They turned around to see Javert who held out his hat smilingly towards them.

Javert had his men stationed behind the trees at nightfall and had entered at the right time. "You shall pass out of the door, and not the window," he ordered. "There are seven of you but fifteen of us."

Javert's men rushed in at his call and bound the bandits. Javert spotted the prisoner now, who had not uttered a word and held his head down.

"Untie monsieur!" Javert ordered and sat down on the table to begin writing his report.

"Bring forward the gentleman whom the bandits had taken prisoner," he ordered his men after some time. The officers looked at each other.

"Where is he?" Javert snapped.

The old man, the prisoner of the bandits, had disappeared.

Chapter Thirteen

The Letter

It was nine in the evening, when Marius slipped out of the house as soon as Javert left with his prisoners. The next morning, he went back, paid his dues and rent, loaded his things on a hand-cart and left without leaving behind an address. Two reasons prompted him to do so; firstly the house terrorized him now, as he had encountered the evil poor there, perhaps even more horrific than the evil rich and secondly, he did not wish to testify against Thenardier in the ensuing trial.

Marius was solely interested now in the fact that he had seen the father of the girl he loved and his only wish was now to reach Ursula.

One day, Eponine, the eldest Thenardier girl, came to Marius's room. She said she had been looking for him for a long time and had the address he had asked her for. Marius followed the girl excitedly.

The house in the deserted Rue Plumet area was a secret house. To the passers-by it seemed to be a two storied-house with a garden of an acre before it. But there was a small yard at the rear of the house and a low building existed at the end of it. This had two rooms and a cellar, enough to hide a few people living there.

In October 1829, a new tenant arrived here quietly with a young girl and an old servant. He repaired the secret passage and the secret doors that ran out to the Rue de Babylone from here. This tenant stole in here silently, rather than someone moving into his own house. His name was Jean Valjean and the young girl was Cosette. But why had Jean Valjean left the convent of the Petit Picpus?

In reality, Jean Valjean was very happy with his life at the convent. But the fact that Cosette would eventually become a nun here, troubled him. He was becoming paternal with each passing day and could not bear the thought of being separated from Cosette. He also felt that the child had the right to know what life was before renouncing it.

The opportunity Jean Valjean awaited came with old Fauchelevent's death. Jean Valjean met the prioress and told her that he had received a small inheritance after his brother's death. This would help him live without work for the rest of his days and he wished to leave the convent with his daughter. He pleaded with the prioress to accept five thousand francs for Cosette's education for five years. Jean Valjean assumed the name of Ultimus Fauchelevent and took the house in the Rue Plumet. He also hired two other lodgings in Paris.

Cosette left the convent when she was fourteen years old and soon blossomed into a beautiful young woman. Marius fell in love with her at first sight and unknown to him, Cosette loved him too. One day, Cosette received an anonymous love letter placed on her garden seat. She immediately knew it was from HIM! That evening as Jean Valjean went out, Marius visited Cosette in her garden and confessed his love for Cosette who returned his love. But Marius was distressed to hear that Cosette's father was planning to take her away to England. He promised to return to meet Cosette in a day.

Jean Valjean planned to leave for England as the police had become very active because of the political troubles. Marius was heartbroken to arrive at Cosette's house and find her missing. Eponine informed Marius that his friends awaited him at the barricade of the Rue de la Chanvrerie. Marius decided to join

the revolutionaries as there was nothing else to live for now. Javert had been captured by the leader of the revolutionaries, Enjolras. He ordered Javert to be shot later as he was a spy of the government.

The Municipal Guards attacked the revolutionaries. Bahorel was killed and Coufeyrac had fallen. As a soldier tried to strike Gavroche dead with his bayonet, a ball struck the soldier in the middle of his forehead. A second ball struck Courfeyrac's assailant in the chest, as a firing Marius entered the barricade. A soldier aimed at Marius but a working-man stepped between the gun and Marius. Marius did not notice as the working man fell. Thanks to Marius, the barricade was redeemed by the revolutionaries and the government forces pushed back. "Where is the chief?" Marius asked, as the others flocked around him. "You are the chief," Enjolras stated. Suddenly, Marius found himself leading the revolutionaries.

Later, Marius discovered a dying Eponine and realized that she was dressed as the working man. Eponine had given up her life by saving his. Before dying, Eponine gave Cosette's letter to Marius, in which she had written to him about leaving for England. Eponine had loved Marius and wanted to separate Cosette from him. Eponine wrote a warning sign to Jean Valjean so that he left Paris with Cosette in a hurry. Eponine dressed as a working man and loitered in Cosette's garden. Cosette gave her a letter to deliver, which she didn't. When Eponine visited Courfeyrac to find Marius, she learnt where the revolutionaries were building the barricade. She had a devious idea; to push both herself and Marius into that death. She led Marius into the barricade but when she saw him about to be killed, she sacrificed her own life to save his. Marius wrote a letter to Cosette and asked Gavroche, the son of Thenardier, to deliver it for him.

After Cosette had written her letter to Marius, she had forgotten her blotter on the sideboard before the mirror. The mirror now reflected her writing and Jean Valjean received a huge shock when he read the words. Stunned, he sank into his armchair. This was the most fearful torture that Jean Valjean had ever received. He immediately guessed that the man was Marius. Informed by the servant that fighting had begun in Paris, Jean Valjean made up his mind.

The boy Gavroche arrived in the Rue de 1'Homme Arme' and was spotted by Jean Valjean.

"Small boy, what is the matter with you?" Jean Valjean asked. "I am hungry, small yourself," Gavroche replied and was stunned when the old man gave him a hundred sous-a-piece. "Could you show me number seven?" Gavroche asked. "What do you want with number seven?" Jean Valjean asked and the boy was silent. An idea flashed in Jean Valjean's

head, and he asked, "Have you brought the letter I'm waiting for?"

"You? You are not a woman!"

"The letter is for Cosette, is it not? I am to deliver it to her. Give it to me."

"You must know then that I'm sent from the barricade?"

"Of course," Jean Valjean replied, and Gavroche handed him the letter.

Jean Valjean rushed upstairs to read Marius's letter. He saw only these words. "*____I die. When you read this, my soul will be near you.*"

Jean Valjean was totally dazzled by these words. He uttered a cry of joy at the death of a hated one. But even after this, he felt gloomy. An hour later, Jean Valjean stepped out as an armed National Guard. He had a loaded musket and cartridges with the help of the porter.

Chapter Fourteen

Jean Valjean to the Rescue

"It is only fair that some of us be given a chance to escape," Enjolras stated and asked how many wanted to go away to join their families, instead of a fight to the death. Five men wanted to leave the ranks.

"There are only four uniforms to mingle with the ranks and escape. Only four can leave," Enjolras stated. The men entrusted upon Marius the responsibility of choosing the four men.

"Me! Me!" all of them shouted at a confused Marius, who was saved from making a difficult decision as Jean Valjean strode in among them wearing his soldier's uniform.

"Who is this man?" Bossuet asked.

"A man who saves others," Combeferre replied.

"I know him," Marius said gravely.

"Welcome citizen," Enjolras addressed Jean Valjean. "You know that we are going to die."

Without replying, Jean Valjean helped the fifth man wear his uniform.

At dawn, a piece of artillery appeared. As the gun sounded and the ball smashed into the barricade, so did Gavroche.

"Proceed!" Bossuet ordered the gunners. Gavroche, the son of Thenardier, was playing a dangerous game. He was picking the cartridge boxes from the dead soldiers. Thanks to his small size and the fog like smoke in the street, he avoided the bullets of the sharpshooters easily. The sight was fascinating and dangerous. Gavroche was being fired at and mocked the firing. The soldiers kept aiming and missing, as Gavroche

lay down, rose up, hid, returned and escaped, making faces at the soldiers who laughed as they shot at him. He filled his basket with cartridge boxes and was singing while the rest of the barricade was trembling. Gavroche was finally felled by a treacherous bullet that was better aimed.

Marius sprang out of the barricade, followed by Combeferre. But they were too late as the boy was dead. Marius brought Gavroche back while Combeferre carried his basket of cartridges. "Alas!" Marius thought. "Thenardier brought back my father alive, while I have brought back his dead son."

Courfeyrac bandaged Marius's forehead with his cravat. A ball had grazed his skull as he had bent to pick up Gavroche.

At noon, Enjolras barked orders. "Fortify the windows in the house with paving stones. Half of the men to the stones and the other half to the muskets."

Marius posted himself on the top of the barricade and kept watch.

"The last man to leave this room will kill this spy," Enjolras added, pointing towards Javert, and laying a pistol on the table. Jean Valjean asked for permission to kill the spy, which was granted. Jean Valjean was left alone with Javert as the others left. He untied Javert and they exited the wine-shop, scaled the wall and landed on the little street.

"Take your revenge," Javert stated, as Jean Valjean took out his knife. To Javert's surprise, he found his bonds cut. "You are free!" Jean Valjean stated. Javert was not a man to be easily surprised but he was stunned now.

"I don't expect to leave this place alive," Jean Valjean continued. "But if I do, I live under the name Fauchelevent, in the Rue de 1' Homme Arme, Number Seven."

"Take care," Javert replied with a scowl.

"Go!"

Javert repeated the address in an undertone and left. Jean Valjean fired the pistol in the air after he was gone.

"It is done!" he said, re-entering the barricade.

The attack, when it happened, resembled a hurricane. Assault after assault struck the barricade and the men who hadn't slept or eaten for more than twenty four hours, still defended the barricade. They were all wounded and armed with ordinary weapons. Yet, the barricade was assaulted and scaled ten times but never taken. Bousset, Feuilly, Courfeyrac, Joly, and Combeferre were all killed. Marius still fought valiantly but was heavily wounded. His face was covered in blood, resembling a red handkerchief, because of a wound on the head.

The final assault happened and succeeded now. Marius fell, as a ball broke his shoulder-blade. In a flash, Jean Valjean was beside Marius. He carried a senseless Marius in his arms and made his way to something that had caught his eye. It was a kind of small well like opening. This was made level with the ground and resembled an iron grating, partially hidden by fallen paving stones. Jean Valjean descended with Marius into this opening, shutting the iron trap door over his head. He discovered that they were in a long underground passage. Jean Valjean was actually in the sewer of Paris. With Marius on his shoulders, he began his journey in complete darkness. After walking for half an hour, he heard the rumble of vehicles over his head.

The police were patrolling the sewers for the revolutionaries on the run and Jean Valjean saw the lantern of the patrol moving about. They had heard a sound but couldn't spot Jean Valjean as he was in the shadows. The sergeant shot at the direction from which the sound had come to reassure the entire patrol. The ball struck the arch just above Jean Valjean's head.

Jean Valjean renewed his laborious advance and as the average height of these arches was five feet six inches, he was forced to bend when he moved forward, so that he did not hit Marius against the arch. It was three o'clock in the afternoon when Jean Valjean reached the belt sewer. Thanks to the light of the air-hole, Jean Valjean bandaged Marius's wounds by tearing open his own shirt and sealed the blood flow. He discovered Marius's pocket-book, in which his name was written on a note, with instructions to carry his corpse to his grandfather in the event of his death. His grandfather's address was also given. Jean Valjean ate the bread he found in Marius's pocket, which refreshed him. Then he put Marius on his back and descended the sewer.

With great difficulty, a fatigued Jean Valjean reached the outlet with an almost dead Marius. But the outlet was closed by a grating secured

with a huge lock. No exit! Jean Valjean's head sunk between his knees beside the motionless Marius. He thought of Cosette.

"Go halves," a low voice said to him as a hand was laid on his shoulder. Jean Valjean saw Thenardier standing beside him who did not recognize Jean Valjean in this state.

"Give me half of what you have taken from the man after killing him," Thenardier stated. "I will let you escape as I have the key."

He displayed the key and in return asked to check the pockets of both Jean Valjean and Marius, discovering thirty francs in total. But instead of taking half, Thenardier took all the money before letting Jean Valjean out.

As soon as they were outside, Jean Valjean laid Marius on the beach and splashed some water on his face. His eyelids did not part but his half-open mouth breathed. Jean Valjean suddenly felt someone standing behind him and turned around to see Javert!

"Who are you?" Javert asked Jean Valjean not recognizing him.

"Jean Valjean," he replied. Javert grabbed his shoulders in a vice like grip immediately.

"Inspector Javert," Jean Valjean stated, like a lion surrendering to the claws of a lynx. "I am your prisoner. In fact, I have never tried to escape you. Please grant me just one thing. Help me carry this man home."

"He is dead!" Javert said. "Who is he?"

"He is alive. His name is Marius and I got him from the barricade," Jean Valjean handed Javert Marius's pocket-book, open at the page penciled by Marius. Javert took it and kept it. Soon, they were in a fiacre moving speedily.

The fiacre arrived at Marius's grandfather's house at nightfall and everyone was asleep. After the house was woken up and Marius deposited there, Jean Valjean had one more request of Javert.

"Let me go home for a moment. Then you can take me anywhere you wish."

But it was Jean Valjean's turn to be surprised as Javert left after depositing him home. Javert took a shortcut towards the Seine River. Leaning with both hands on the parapet, he reflected. To owe his life to a convict and to spare him in return, had astonished Javert. Javert also felt immense admiration for Jean Valjean. Respect for a galley-slave? How was that possible? How could he neglect his duty and spare a convict as an act of kindness? This internal struggle in Javert's heart broke him and he looked down below at the rapids of Seine and arrived at a decision. Javert jumped into the waters below!

Marius was declared out of danger by the physician after a struggle of four months. The damaged relations between him and his grandfather had been mended. As the old saying goes, a father might hate his son but a grandfather always loves his grandson. The old

man swallowed his foolish pride and gladly consented when Marius wished to marry Cosette. M. Gillenormand liked Cosette at first sight and it helped the cause when Jean Valjean gave Cosette five hundred and eighty-four thousand francs as a wedding gift.

This was whatever Jean Valjean had made as Monsieur Madeleine. He had buried this sum in a forest in Montfermeil. All of Marius's efforts to locate Thenardier went in vain. All he knew that the Thenardiess had died in prison. Marius also did not know who had saved him from certain death, although he had tried his best to do so. Jean Valjean never disclosed that he was the one.

Chapter Fifteen

The Sacrifice

The day after Marius and Cosette were married, Jean Valjean decided to see Marius. He confessed to Marius that he was an old convict, a galley-slave and not Cosette's natural father. By this action, Jean Valjean distanced himself from both Marius and Cosette. Naturally, Marius was repulsed by Jean Valjean now and gradually removed all physical traces of him, by banishing him from the house. But one thing Marius couldn't explain. Why had the old man entered the barricade? Marius naturally assumed that he had done so to kill Javert. He did not know that Javert had committed suicide, much later.

One day, the portress of Jean Valjean discovered that the old man was very sick. He had stayed in bed for a full week. She called the physician and asked him what was wrong with the old man, after he had examined him.

"He is a man who seems to have lost a dear friend," the physician replied. "People die of that."

"Will you come again, doctor?" she asked.

"Yes, but another than I, must come again," he replied.

One evening, Jean Valjean had great difficulty in raising himself upon his elbow. He found no pulse when he felt his wrist and his breathing was short and laboured. He realized that he was weaker than ever before. Jean Valjean raised himself with a supreme effort. He took out Cosette's things, examined them and cried. He looked into the mirror and clearly saw the mark of death. Night arrived and Jean Valjean fainted with the effort of writing a letter to Cosette. He was thirsty when he regained consciousness and could not lift the water pitcher. With a great effort, he tipped it towards his mouth, to drink a swallow. He wrote a few lines and stopped. The pen dropped from his fingers and his body shook with sobs.

"Oh Cosette! It's all over. My God! I shall never see her again!" he exclaimed pitifully. That very moment, there was a rap at his door.

That evening, Marius was informed in his office that a man named Thenard wished to see him. His letter stated that he possessed a secret regarding a particular individual who could harm Monsieur Baron's family. Marius asked for the man to be sent in and he entered.

"Monsieur Baron, you have a robber and an assassin in your house," he stated. "His name is Jean Valjean."

"I am aware of it," Marius replied.

"He is an old convict."

"I know it."

The stranger smiled. "I have a secret concerning the fortune of Madame the Baroness. I offer it for only twenty thousand francs."

"I know that secret as well as the others," Marius replied.

"Ten thousand francs," the man lowered his price. Marius shook his head, and the man went as low as twenty francs now.

"I know Jean Valjean's secret as well as yours," Marius stated to the man. "I also know your name."

"Of course you do, Monsieur Baron. I have had the honor of writing and telling you that it is Thenard."

"Thenardier!" Marius declared.

"Who is that?"

"I have told you your name, Thenardier and I also know your secrets," Marius declared. "I have my means of information. I know that Jean Valjean is a robber because he robbed a rich manufacturer, M. Madeleine. I know he is an assassin as he murdered the police-officer, Javert."

"You are on the wrong track, Monsieur Baron," Thenardier insisted. "Jean Valjean never robbed M. Madeleine and he never killed Javert."

"How is that?"

"Jean Valjean did not rob M. Madeleine as he was M. Madeleine himself and he did not kill Javert as Javert committed suicide."

"Prove it!" Marius cried and Thenardier produced the necessary documents in the form of newspaper cuttings to prove what he said was true. After he read the old newspaper cuttings, Marius was beside himself with joy.

"This unhappy man is a hero!" he exclaimed. "He is Madeleine, the providence of an entire region! He is a saint!"

"He's not a saint or a hero," Thenardier protested. "He is an assassin and a robber! He killed a man in the Grand Sewer of Paris about a year ago, on the 6th of June, 1832."

Marius appeared terribly interested at this revelation and Thenardier continued, "A man spotted Jean Valjean in the sewer carrying a corpse. This man had the key out of the sewer and had to give it to the convict as he possessed great strength. The man in the sewer was none other than me and I was witness to the fact that Jean Valjean was carrying the young man he had murdered."

"That young man was none other than me," Marius declared, as he stood up angrily. "Jean Valjean did not kill me but saved my life!"

Thenardier was scared now but Marius threw thousand francs at Thenardier. "You are the one who's a robber and an assassin Thenardier," he thundered. "Go away with this money. Leave this place. Go to Waterloo as it protects you. You saved the life of a colonel there. You

will depart for America with your daughter. I shall give you twenty thousand francs and see that you leave to get hung elsewhere."

"Eternal gratitude, Monsieur Baron," Thenardier bowed and took his leave. He left for America two days later, under a false name with his daughter. Now, Marius ran to Cosette and informed her that her father was the one who had saved his life. Together, they left for Jean Valjean's residence immediately.

Chapter Sixteen

The Death of a Hero

Jean Valjean turned his head at the knock on the door.

"Come in," he said weakly. Cosette and Marius rushed into the room.

"Father!" Cosette exclaimed as she fell upon Jean Valjean's chest.

"Cosette? Oh my God!" the old man exclaimed in joy, as he rose up. "Is it you?"

"Father!" Marius stepped forward and whispered, trying not to cry.

"You forgive me then?" Jean Valjean asked and Marius did not, could not, reply.

"Thanks," the old man added.

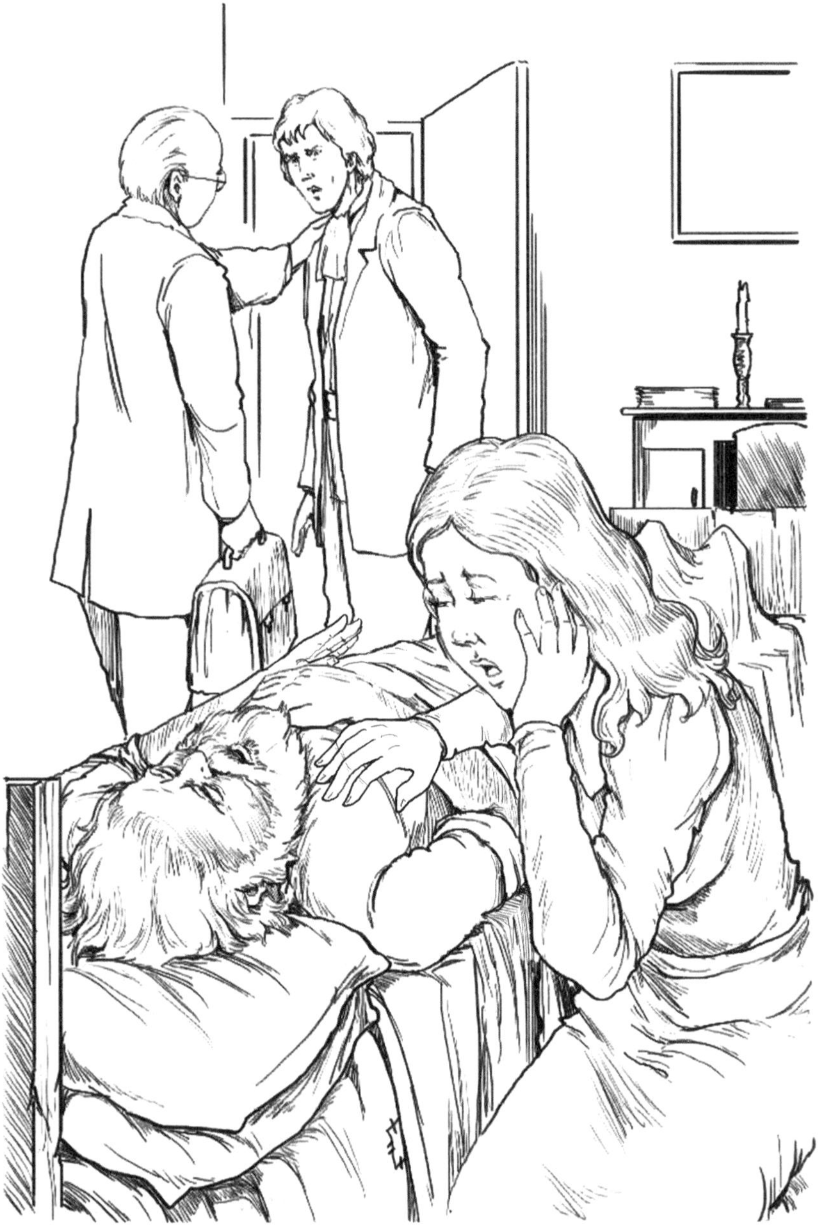

"Cosette, do you hear?" Marius exclaimed. "That is the way with him. He saves my life and begs my pardon. He sacrificed himself for us and he thanks an ungrateful man like myself. Cosette, your father is an angel!"

"Hush! Why say all that?" Jean Valjean whispered.

"Why did you not say you were Monsieur Madeleine? Why did you not say that you saved Javert's life? Why didn't you tell me I owe my life to you? You shall never leave us again now."

"I shall die in a few minutes," Jean Valjean whispered, and Cosette and Marius shuddered. As they pleaded with the old man, the physician arrived. He examined Jean Valjean and whispered into Marius's ear, "Too late!"

Jean Valjean grew weaker by the minute. He summoned Cosette and Marius closer. It was clearly the last minute of his last hour.

"I love you two dearly," Jean Valjean declared. "The money I leave behind is honest money.

I have left a letter behind in which the details of my business are given. I must confess that I have not always loved you, Monsieur Pontmercy. But now I think of you and Cosette as one and love you dearly. I have a five hundred franc bill in my bureau. It is for the poor. Forgive the wicked Thenardiers! Cosette, your mother's name was Fantine! Fall on your knees whenever you pronounce it. She suffered so much and loved you so much. I am going away now, children. Love each other dearly always. Think of me a little. Come nearer, and let me die happy. Let me put my hands upon your dear beloved heads."

Cosette and Marius fell on their knees, overwhelmed and choked with tears. Each grabbed one of the old man's hands. But sadly, those august hands moved no more. Jean Valjean was dead!

Chapter Seventeen

Les Misérables

In the cemetery of Pere Lachaise, in the neighborhood of Potter's field, far away from the elegant *quartier* of the city of sepulchers, far away from those fantastic tombs, in a deserted corner, beside an old wall, among the dog-grass and the mosses, there lies a stone. The leprosy of time, the mould, the lichen and the bird droppings have not spared this stone. The air has turned it black and the water, green. It is not near any path and people do not come here because the grass is high and they would wet their feet. The lizards emerge when there is a little sunshine and there is a rustling of wild

oats all about. In the spring, the linnets sing in the tree.

This particular stone is entirely blank. The only thought in cutting it was as per the wishes of the dead man, to consist of the essentials of the grave; there was no other care than to make this stone long enough and narrow enough to cover a man.

That headstone remains nameless.

About the Author

■ George Elliot

Victor Marie Hugo (26 February 1802 - 22 May 1885) was a French poet, novelist, and dramatist of the Romantic Movement. Hugo is considered one of the greatest and best-known French writers. His most famous works are the novels Les Misérables, 1862 and The Hunchback of Notre-Dame, 1831.

Victor Hugo was born on February 26, 1802 in Besançon, France to mother Sophie Trébuche and father Joseph-Léopold-Sigisbert Hugo. His father was a military officer who later served as a general under Napoleon. After training as a lawyer, Hugo embarked on the literary career. Hugo died on May 22, 1885 in Paris.

Les Misérables was published in 1862 and was a huge success. Later reinterpreted as a theatrical musical and a film. Les Misérables remains one of the best-known works of 19th century literature.

■ List of Main Characters

Jean Valjean - Cosette's adopted father, Jean Valjean is an ex-convict who makes his fortune with innovative industrial techniques. He finds fulfillment in loving his adopted daughter and helping people in difficult situations.

Cosette - Fantine's daughter and Valjean's adopted daughter, after her mother dies; Cosette spends her childhood as a servant for the Thénardiers till she is rescued by Valjean. She finds fulfillment in her love for Marius.

Javert - A police inspector who strictly believes in law and order. Javert nurses an especially strong desire to recapture Valjean, whose escape and prosperity he sees as an affront to justice.

Fantine - A working class girl who leaves her hometown to seek her fortune in Paris. Fantine's innocent affair leaves her pregnant and abandoned. But she makes a Herculean effort to feed herself and her daughter, Cosette.

Marius - The son of Georges Pontmercy, a colonel in Napoléon's army, Marius grows up in the home of his grandfather. Marius has an identity crisis when he learns the real reason for his separation from his father, and tries discovering himself. He falls in love with Cosette.

M. Myriel - The bishop of Digne. M. Myriel is a much-admired clergyman with great kindness and charity. He passes on these same qualities to Valjean and initiates the ex-convict's spiritual renewal.

M. Thénardier - A cruel, wretched, money obsessed man who first appears as Cosette's keeper and tormentor. His schemes range from extortion to robbery to fraud to murder.

■ Questions

Chapter 1

- *Describe the stranger who walked into the town of D___?*
- *Describe what happened when the traveller knocked on the peasant's door?*

Chapter 2

- *Describe the conversation between the convict and the Bishop?*
- *Why was the convict surprised at the end of the conversation?*

Chapter 3

- *Briefly describe Jean Valjean's early life.*
- *What was the incident that led to Jean Valjean's arrest?*

Chapter 4

- *Who were the four men who arrived to see the Bishop? Why?*
- *Do you find Bishop Myriel's kindness believable? Why or why not?*

Chapter 5

- *Describe the vehicle that was used as a place for swinging by the little girls.*
- *What bargain did Fantine strike with the Thenardiers?*

Chapter 6

- *How did Father Madeleine become the Mayor?*
- *How responsible is Jean Valjean for his financial success? How responsible is Bishop Myriel for it?*

Chapter 7

- *Who was Javert? Describe in detail.*
- *Why was Javert so committed to catching Jean Valjean?*

Chapter 8

- *Why did Jean Valjean attend the trial of Champmathieu?*
- *How was Champmathieu proven innocent?*

Chapter 9

- *Describe how Fantine died?*
- *Why did Jean Valjean's arrest cause a sensation? Why didn't people support him?*

Chapter 10

- *How did Jean Valjean escape?*
- *How did Jean Valjean and Fauchelevant convince the prioress and the reverend mother to allow Jean and Cosette to stay at the convent?*

Chapter 11

- *How did Marius come to love the father he once hated? Describe.*
- *What are the central conflicts that lead Marius to leave Gillenormand's house?*

Chapter 12

- *Why was Marius shocked when he heard the name 'Thenardier'? Explain in detail.*
- *How did Marius save the old man from certain death?*

Chapter 13

- *Who was Gavroche? What job did Marius entrust him with?*
- *Why do you think Gavroche is one of the most memorable characters in French literature?*

Chapter 14

- *How does Javert react when Jean Valjean saves his life? Why? What does it tell us about the theme of justice in this book?*
- *What ultimately drove Javert to suicide? Describe the incident.*

Chapter 15

- *Who was the stranger that came to see Marius? Why?*
- *What was the outcome of this meeting? Describe in detail.*

Chapter 16

- *Why did Marius think that Jean Valjean was an angel?*
- *What did Jean Valjean tell Cosette about her mother in his last words?*

Chapter 17

- *Which character do you have the least sympathy for? Why?*
- *What main lesson do you take away from Les Misérables? Is it a convincing one? Why or why not?*